Paddington At the Seaside was
first published in Great Britain by
William Collins Sons and Co Ltd.
This edition published in 1992 by HarperCollins Publishers Ltd
Reprinted 1992
Text © Michael Bond 1972
Illustrations © HarperCollins Publishers Ltd 1992

A CIP catalogue record for this book is available
from the British Library

ISBN 0 00 193665 4

Printed and bound in The Peoples Republic of China

Paddington at the Seaside

Michael Bond

Illustrated by John Lobban

HarperCollins*Publishers*

"Today," said Mr Brown at breakfast one bright,
summer morning, "feels like the kind of day for
taking a young bear to the seaside. Hands up all
those who agree."

Jonathan, Judy and Mrs Brown all put up their hands. And Paddington raised both of his paws as well, just to make sure.

Everyone was very excited, and by the time they set out the Browns' car was so full of things there was hardly room to move.

Paddington carefully fastened his safety belt, and then peered out of the window as he felt the car turn a corner.

"Are we nearly there, Mr Brown?" he asked hopefully.

Mr Brown removed a spade handle from his left ear. "I'm afraid not," he said gloomily. "We've only just left Windsor Gardens, and it's a very long way to the sea."

Mr Brown was right. It *was* a long journey. But when they reached the seaside the sight of the sand and the water soon made up for it.

Paddington gave an excited sniff as he climbed out of the car. Even the air had a different smell.

"That's because it's special seaside air," said Mrs Brown. "It's very good for you."

Paddington looked round anxiously as Mr Brown began laying out the beach things.

"I hope all the air doesn't get used up, Mrs Brown," he said in a loud voice. And he gave a man who was doing some deep-breathing exercises a very hard stare indeed.

"Come on, Paddington," called Judy. "Let's go for a swim."

It took Paddington some while to get ready. He wasn't the sort of bear who believed in taking chances and by the time he went in the sea he was wearing so many things he promptly sank.

"No wonder!" cried Judy, as she went to his rescue. "You haven't even bothered to blow up your paw-bands!"

"Fancy wearing a duffle-coat!" exclaimed Jonathan.

"I thought the water might be cold," gasped Paddington.

After his paw-bands had been properly blown up
Paddington went in the water again, and with some
help from Jonathan and Judy he was soon
swimming very well indeed.

After his swim Paddington settled down in a deckchair in order to dry out.

He had hardly closed his eyes when he heard something very strange going on behind him.

First there was a loud cry.

Then there was the sound of people booing.

"They're watching Mr Briggs' Punch and Judy," explained Mrs Brown.

Paddington jumped up and looked at the others as if
he could hardly believe his ears. But Mr and Mrs
Brown seemed much too busy with the picnic things
to be bothered, so he turned and hurried up the
beach towards the spot where the noise was
coming from.

"Where's Paddington?" asked Jonathan, when he and Judy arrived back shortly afterwards carrying some ice creams.

"I hope he won't be long," said Judy. "I've got him a special giant cone. He'll be most upset if it all melts."

Jonathan glanced up and down the beach. "Crikey!" he said suddenly. "Look over there!"

The Browns gave a gasp as they turned to follow the
direction of Jonathan's gaze.

Something very odd seemed to be going on inside
the Punch and Judy tent
    There was a large bulge in one side and it was
heaving up and down almost as it if was alive.

Suddenly the tent began moving across the sand,
scattering people in all directions. It just missed a
large sand castle, went twice round the ice cream
man and then headed towards the sea.

"Quick!" shouted Judy. "Let's cut it off!"

But she was too late.

"Paddington!" cried Judy, as a familiar figure swam into view. "What on earth are you doing? That's the second time I've had to rescue you!"

Paddington stared at her in amazement. "But I
went to rescue *you*!" he exclaimed. "Mrs Brown said
you were being punched by Mr Briggs."

Mrs Brown looked at Paddington in astonishment. Then her face cleared.

"I didn't say Mr Briggs was *punching* Judy," she explained. "I said it was his Punch *and* Judy."

"It's a puppet theatre," said Judy. "They often have them at the seaside. There's one puppet called Mr Punch, and when he gets cross all the audience have to boo."

If it took the Browns a long time to explain a Punch and Judy show to Paddington, it took them even longer to explain Paddington to Mr Briggs.

But when he saw the enormous crowd watching them from the promenade his face lit up. It was the biggest audience he'd had for a long time and he decided to make the most of it and put another show on there and then.

"You can have a seat in the front row," he said to Paddington. "I expect bears do very good boos."

One way and another Paddington enjoyed his day out at the seaside. But all good things come to an end, and when it was time to leave he stood for a moment holding up an empty marmalade jar.

"I'm just collecting some sea air for the journey home," he announced.

"I think I shall sleep so well on the way back I may lose all of today's air with my snores!"